"Wait for me!" Said Maggie McGee

by Jean Van Leeuwen · pictures by Jacqueline Rogers

PHYLLIS FOGELMAN BOOKS · NEW YORK

Published by Phyllis Fogelman Books
An imprint of Penguin Putnam Books for Young Readers
345 Hudson Street
New York, New York 10014

Designed by Atha Tehon and Kimi Weart
Text set in Greco-Roman
Printed in Hong Kong on acid-free paper
1 3 5 7 9 10 8 6 4 2

Library of Congress Cataloging-in-Publication Data
Van Leeuwen, Jean.
"Wait for me!" said Maggie McGee/by Jean Van Leeuwen;
pictures by Jacqueline Rogers.
p.   cm.
Summary: There are lots of disadvantages to being
the smallest in her family—not being able to ride a bike, play basketball,
or go to school—but after a long wait, Maggie grows up.
ISBN 0-8037-2357-1
[1. Brothers and sisters—Fiction. 2. Growth—Fiction.]
I. Rogers, Jacqueline, ill. II. Title.
PZ7.V275 Wai 2001
[E]—dc21   00-026953

Thanks again to Gordon Fitting and all the great
staff, faculty, and students at Chatham Middle School.
J. R.

*The art for this book was done in watercolor on
Winsor & Newton watercolor paper.*

To my aunt Ruth
J. V. L.

For my siblings, Marcy, Bobby, Janet, Lucy, and Martin,
from your littlest Jackie
J. R.

In the McGee family
there were Benny and Lenny

and Willy

and Lily

and Ruby

and Maxie and Maisie.

And last and littlest
was Maggie.

Maggie was too little to reach the table, unless she sat on two phone books.

She was too little to reach the pedals of her red tricycle.

She was too little to reach the cookies.

And when Benny and Lenny and Willy and Lily and Ruby and Maxie and
Maisie left each morning, singing, "Hi ho, hi ho, it's off to school we go,"
Maggie sadly waved good-bye.

All day she waited.

When they finally came home, she ran after them.

"Wait for me!" called Maggie.

But they didn't wait. By the time she caught up, they were finishing their snack. Maggie got the piece of cake with no icing.

Then they went off to ride bikes.
("Wait for me!" cried Maggie.)
    Or climb trees.
("Are you *ever* coming down?" asked Maggie.)

Or play ball. ("Can I play, please, please, PLEASE?" begged Maggie.)
Sometimes, when they lost the ball, they let Maggie find it.

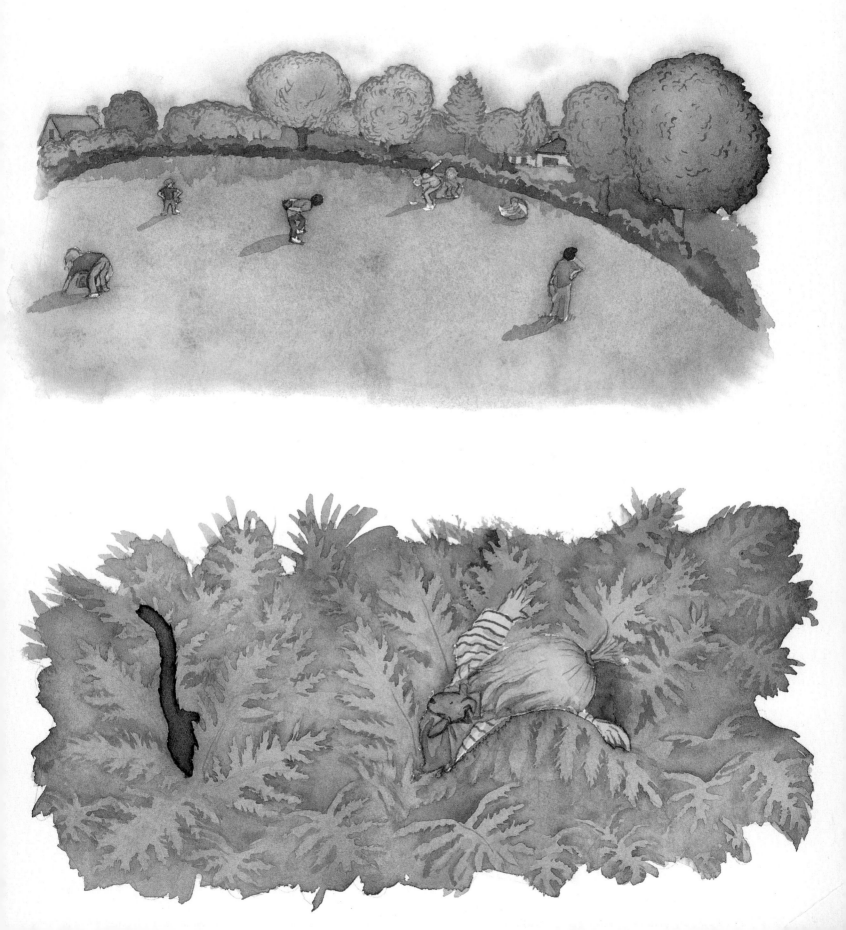

Being the littlest, Maggie got to wear Benny and Lenny and Willy and Lily and Ruby and Maxie and Maisie's hand-me-downs. Only by the time they got to her, they were all worn out. Willy's overalls smelled like frog. Lily's ballet shoes had holes in the toes. And they never handed down the good stuff, like Lily's tutu or Maxie's drums or the Grand and Glorious Wizard costume.

Maggie was a pumpkin
three Halloweens
in a row.

While Maggie was doing all that waiting, she found things. A perfectly round, perfectly white pebble. A bird's nest. Lenny's lost homework. A frog. She put everything in Willy's froggy overalls with all the pockets.

And while she was waiting, she was stretching. And bouncing. And growing.

Until finally she was big enough
to sit at the table
without a phone book.

And ride her red tricycle.

And, on tippy toes, reach the cookies.
Finally she was ready for school.
Now, thought Maggie,
I am big like everybody else.

Her mother made her a dress with lots of pockets so she could take all her things for Show-and-Tell. She had a lunch box, and two sharp pencils ready for homework. When Benny and Lenny and Willy and Lily and Ruby and Maxie and Maisie left for school, she went too.

"Wait for me!" shouted Maggie. And this time they did.

School was wonderful. Maggie was a star at Show-and-Tell. She gave herself homework even when the teacher didn't. And she wasn't the littlest anymore. In fact, she was next to the biggest in her whole class.

But not big enough.

At recess the big kids got to play on the Super Duper Climbing Castle.
The little kids got to play on the baby swings.

The big kids got to make announcements to the whole school. "Attention, students!" they said. The little kids got to listen.

The big kids got to play loud, shiny instruments like trumpets and tubas.
The little kids played kazoos.

The big kids got to go on a camping trip and sleep in real tents, and Willy brought home a real (maybe) dinosaur bone. The little kids went to the zoo. Again.

After school Maggie came home with Benny and Lenny and Willy and Lily and Ruby and Maxie and Maisie.
They rode bikes. And climbed trees. And played ball.

Only now all Benny and Lenny wanted
to play was basketball, and the hoop
was so high that Maggie could never,
ever possibly make a basket. I will
never be big enough, thought Maggie.
Not in my whole life.

The sign on stage reads:

SLEEPING
BEAUTY
AND THE
BEANSTALK
BY
THE FOURTH GRADE

Then one day the fourth grade put on its play, "Sleeping Beauty and the Beanstalk." It was a fairy tale they made up themselves. Willy played the handsome prince. Maggie sat in the front row with all the little kids.

It didn't take long to see that Willy was in trouble. He had practiced his lines a hundred times at home. But now, he forgot.

"Oh, thank you, Fairy Godmother," said Willy. "For..." And then he stopped.

"For granting my three wishes," whispered Maggie.

"What?" said Willy.

"FOR GRANTING MY THREE WISHES, SILLY!" shouted Maggie.
Everyone laughed.

Finally the prince and princess climbed down the beanstalk. But before they
could live happily ever after, they had to see if the glass slipper fit.

"Hey," said Willy. "Where is it?" The seven dwarfs looked everywhere.
But they couldn't find it.

The princess looked like she was going to cry.

Luckily, Maggie had brought Lily's ballet shoes for Show-and-Tell.
She climbed up on stage. "You can borrow one of these," she said.

The shoe fit. The prince and princess rode off to live happily ever after.
Then the curtain came down and the players took a bow. And so did Maggie,
high up on stage with everyone clapping and cheering.

Never in her whole life had she felt so big.

"You saved our play," said the princess.

"You should get three wishes," said the fairy godmother.

"Anything you want," said Willy.

So the next day Maggie went to the principal's office. She had to stand on her tippy toes to reach the microphone.

"Attention, students!" she announced. "This is Maggie."

After school she played basketball with Benny and Lenny and Willy and
Lily and Ruby and Maxie and Maisie. Benny and Lenny took turns holding
her on their shoulders and she made twenty-seven baskets. She even got to dunk.
"And now for your third wish," said Willy.
But Maggie shook her head. "I can't tell," she said. "It's a secret."

It took a long time, but finally finally finally Maggie's third wish came true. She grew up to be bigger than Benny and Lenny and Willy and Lily and Ruby and Maxie and Maisie. In fact, she was the biggest in the whole McGee family. And really good at basketball.